JOURNEY

THE STORY OF A THERAPY HORSE

Lisa Chambers & Jennifer Walters
Illustrated by Karelyn Siegler

Library of Congress Control Number: 2015951076

Printed in China
First edition 1 2016
This product conforms to CPSIA 2008
ISBN: 9781934860069

For Sarah, Penny, and Dude — Lisa and Jennifer

For Mom, the first artist that I have ever watched make a beautiful picture.
For my niece Avery, who interviewed me for her class project and chose me as her favorite illustrator.
For my agent Janet, who made all this possible and can always see into the heart of a matter.
And lastly to Malc and The Bear who just make life better. — Karelyn

On a starry night in a country backyard, a colt was born.
A little girl watched as his mother licked him clean.

Then, as foals must, he struggled to stand. He fell. Once, twice, three times. Finally, he lurched onto his wobbly legs and stood.

"Hooray!" exclaimed the girl.

"What will you call him?" her father asked.

The girl's head tipped back as she thought, and she gazed at the night sky.

"Star" she said, and smiled.

Just like Star, the girl was small, but they grew together. Every day she rushed to the barn. She curried Star's coat and picked out his hooves. She threw sweet-smelling hay down from the loft. Sometimes, as she softly brushed dust from his face, she whispered secrets to him that no one else knew.

Star learned to accept a bridle and bit, and even the snug girth of the saddle around his belly. The girl taught him to walk, trot, and canter on cue. Together they sailed over cross-poles. They won many ribbons, and the girl decorated her bedroom with them.

For years, Star lived happily in the only home he'd ever known, with the girl who loved him best. Then one day, the girl, who was no longer little, trudged into the barn. She slid open the stall door and reached for her horse.

"I'm going away to school," she told him as tears spilled onto his cheek. "You can't stay here by yourself. I will find you a new home."

Soon a woman came to meet Star. She ran her hands down his legs and studied him from every angle. She lunged him in circles and watched how he moved. Then she swung onto his back and rode around the yard.

"He's a nice horse. He'll do just fine," the woman said as she led him to her trailer. With ears pricked and nostrils flared, Star climbed up the ramp. Then the doors clanged shut, and the trailer bumped down the drive.

At his new home, Star did not compete in shows, and no one called him Star. The lesson barn already owned a horse by that name, so he was called Scout instead. Every day, girls and boys came to learn how to ride. Scout stood still as their little hands brushed his back and played with his mane. He gobbled up the treats they brought him. But Scout didn't like the lessons. His riders were unsteady. Some were afraid. One even fell off. Unsure, Scout would stop and refuse to move until the woman marched over and led him herself. Soon no one wanted to ride Scout.

One evening, the woman stepped into his stall and sighed. "I can't keep a lesson horse that no one rides." She led Scout to the trailer, and he climbed inside. Once again he rumbled off toward a new home.

It was a stable for trail riding, miles away. Day after day, Scout walked a path through the trees. The people who came to ride called him Dude, because that was the name stamped on his handed-down saddle. When midday heat scorched Dude's coat and lather appeared at his girth, he trudged along with the other horses. At night, he shared a field with them, and he became one of the herd.

Then one morning, no one came to ready them for their work. Instead, trucks and trailers rolled in. Horses were culled out and taken away. One, two, five, ten... then all the others were gone, except Dude. He waited alone in the big field. Days passed, but no one else came. He ate the grass until it was gone. He sipped murky water from the creek. He stripped bark from trees and tried to eat it.

Finally, one evening, a truck crept up the path. Dude lifted his head. A man climbed out and walked toward the horse. "It looks like they forgot you," he said. He ran a hand down Dude's thin neck. "You must be pretty hungry." The man snapped a lead rope to the gelding's muddy halter and led him away.

At his new home, Dude was nursed back to health. Gradually, his ribs were hidden by flesh, and his coat began to shine. The owner of the stable was pleased. She thought Dude could work as a therapy horse, helping people with special needs. But he would have to pass many tests first.

Dude was led back and forth, round and round, while horse handlers and therapists studied his gait. They rattled toys at him and rolled balls under his belly. They led him to wheelchairs and walkers so he could see them from every angle. People sat sideways, backwards, and even stood on his back. Dude never shied.

"He's smart and sound and just the right size," the stable manager told the owner. They agreed he would stay.

"What will we call him?" she asked.

The man stepped back to study the horse. "He's walked many trails," he said. "Let's call him Journey."

Journey became a therapy horse. He stood still at the mounting block as therapists guided kids onto his back. Their muscles were strengthened as they reached for his ears and played games on the move. Helpers walked on either side of Journey to keep the kids safe as they balanced above him with their arms stretched wide. Soon sitting tall and walking up the ramp became easier for his riders. They did things they'd never been able to do, and Journey was there beneath them, warm and steady.

One day, a little girl came to ride Journey. The therapist helped her walk to him because her legs were wobbly. She sat on his back and laughed and spoke out loud, though nobody understood her mixed-up words. When their work was finished, the therapist helped her down from the horse.

The girl giggled when his nose touched hers, and she laid her head on his cheek. She gently brushed dust from his face and whispered secrets to him that no one else knew. Journey closed his eyes and listened.